Warren Ellis
WRITER

▾

Ken Lashley
(CHAPTERS 1, 3, 4)
Roger Cruz & Renato Arlem
(CHAPTER 2)
PENCILERS

▾

Tom Wegrzyn, Phillip Moy,
Bud Larosa, Harry Candelario
INKERS

▾

Joe Rosas
COLORIST

▾

Richard Starkings/Comicraft
LETTERERS

▾

SUZANNE GAFFNEY
EDITOR/DESIGNER

BOB HARRAS
EDITOR IN CHIEF

Carlos
Pacheco &
Cam Smith
X-CALIBRE #1
COVER ▾

Carlos
Pacheco &
Bill
Sienkiewicz
X-CALIBRE #3
COVER ▾

ULTIMATE X-CALIBRE™ Originally
published in magazine form as X-Calibre
#'s 1-4. Published by Marvel Comics,
387 Park Avenue South, New York, New
York 10016. Copyright © 1995 Marvel
Entertainment Group, Inc. All rights
reserved. X-Men, X-Calibre, and all
prominent characters appearing herein
and the distinctive names and likenesses
thereof are trademarks of Marvel Entertainment Group, Inc. No part of this book
may be printed or reproduced in any
manner without the written permission
of the publisher. ISBN #0-7851-0132-2
Printed in Canada. GST #R127032852.
First Printing: May, 1995.

10 9 8 7 6 5 4 3 2 1

The pole drops through the glassy water, pushing past the thousands of crystalline shards of ice that hang in the river...

...slowly propelling the ferry back towards the ruthless colors of the funereal world outside.

Here, under low stone, in the greens and greys of a magical new world, is the **unknown**.

They called her SWITCHBACK, home in DETROIT under the makeshift rooves where the sacred street mutants once huddled...

She's made her leap of faith now. Freezing and frightened, she doesn't know what happens next.

But she's a million miles away from home, and she's never going back there again.

The monolith in sackcloth does not speak again for the rest of the day.

SWITCHBACK'S quest seems neverending. She thought, after the trek from AMERICA that killed all her companions —

— don't think about them, not about GARY, his hand on her cheek, his lifeless body adrift in the water —

— she thought she'd made it. But no. It goes on.

Her bones hurt. The forest canopy blocks the light she needs to take the frost out of her muscles.

It's even worse at night. The meager fire the monk scratched together doesn't begin to help.

The monk, CAIN, doesn't seem to feel the weather.

HOW IS IT?

IT'S RIDICULOUSLY COLD, THE FIRE WOULDN'T ROAST A RAT IF YOU DANGLED THE BUGGER IN THE FLAMES FOR A YEAR —

— THESE'RE THE ONLY CLOTHES I HAVE AN' THERE'S STILL ICE IN 'EM, AND I'M STUCK IN A FOREST WITH AN INANE RELIGIOUS FREAK ON STEROIDS.

THAT ABOUT COVER IT?

I MEANT *THE WORLD OUT-SIDE.*

HOW *IS* IT?

WORSE.

I *SEE.*

WE MUST *CONTINUE.*

AW, MAN...

They trudge on.

SWITCHBACK doesn't know whether to laugh or cry when *CAIN* starts jabbering, tranced, about some dead brother of his.

Hours bleed into days, and she doesn't notice the mud getting warmer and wetter...

...not until it's almost upon her...

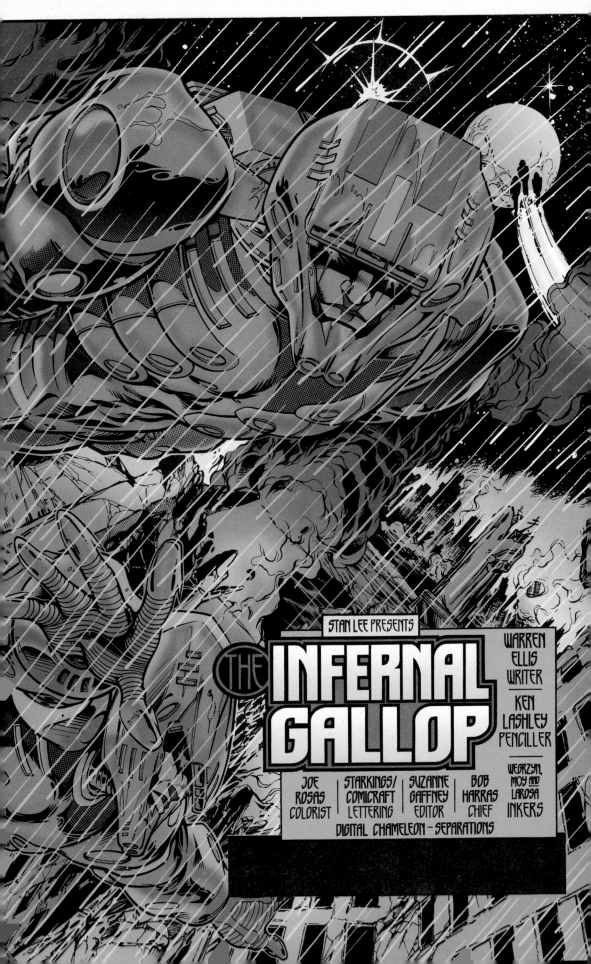

STAN LEE PRESENTS

THE INFERNAL GALLOP

WARREN ELLIS WRITER

KEN LASHLEY PENCILLER

WEGRZYN, MOY AND LAROSA INKERS

JOE ROSAS COLORIST

STARKINGS/ COMICRAFT LETTERING

SUZANNE GAFFNEY EDITOR

BOB HARRAS CHIEF

DIGITAL CHAMELEON - SEPARATIONS

Vaulting from the wet gridwork of uptown is the nightclub *HEAVEN*;

HEAVEN

Only a soundless few appreciate the black, cold-blooded joke of the name.

The man who **thought** of it can, these days, barely summon any reaction to it.

WARREN WORTHINGTON, who has sold any piece of him worth keeping to make Heaven what it is.

This is the cost of holding a sliver of heaven in the guts of hell, then;

PRIVATE

Having no soul left to enjoy it with.

WORTHINGTON.

HAVE THE ARRANGEMENTS BEEN *MADE?* OR MUST I BECOME...

...*ANNOYED?*

The dirty rain finally stops falling in Manhattan.

But the alien heat of the damaged climate evaporates the black puddles, and the city grows smothered in stinking cess-colored fog...

Stench and orders stop KURT DARKHOLME from wasting time forcing boards or hunting secret doors.

BAMF

BAMF

Inside, the explosive reek of teleportation mixes with the compost and salt of rotting wood...

...and dust and incense...

THAT'S *ASININE*.

WE'RE ALL LOOKING FOR SOMETHING TO HOPE FOR, DARKHOLME.

YOU KNOW MY NAME?

ALL OF US WORKING ON THE *INFERNAL GALLOP*, THIS *REFUGEE PIPELINE* FROM HERE TO *AVALON*, KNOW ABOUT THE *DARKHOLMES*.

WE *KNOW* HOW YOUR MOTHER STRIPS *EVERYTHING OF WORTH* FROM HER TRANSPORTEES BEFORE DOING HER *JOB*.

WE DON'T *LIKE* HER. WE DON'T LIKE *YOU*.

MY MOTHER *DOES* HER JOB. WHAT *MORE* DO YOU WANT?

HONESTY! *DECENCY!* THIS IS A *HOLY CHORE* WE DO! DON'T AVOID THE *POINT!*

BAMF

EEEYAAA!

The edge of Manhattan.

The submarine, its decrepit stealth machinery groaning and grinding, slides from beneath *GHOST DANCE* into the poisoned *HUDSON*.

Nearly a hundred refugees huddle in the cramped, icy cargo bay, locked into an uncertain future.

And *KURT DARKHÖLME.*

He's thinking about his mother.

He's thinking that if half the things they say are quarter true of her...

AMERICA IS DEAD.

What sits in its place is a gangrenous wound of a nation -- the American dream of the creature **APOCALYPSE.**

These altered states of America have become a staging area for Apocalypse's next, best nightmare -- the corruption of the rest of the **WORLD.**

The troubled dissident movement within America has, until recently, been fighting a losing battle, outmatched and riven by internal dispute. Now, with the discovery of a man purporting to be from an **ALTERNATE TIMELINE,** they move with new purpose.

KURT DARKHOLME, guerilla fighter with the revolutionary band named X-MEN, has been dispatched by cell leader MAGNETO to locate the woman named DESTINY. Her talent of psychometric clairvoyancy -- literally, to touch someone and see their future -- will validate the alternate man's claims.

To effect this, Darkholme has begun a dangerous journey along the refugee pipeline from America to Antarctica and the secret mutant refuge of AVALON...where his MOTHER ferries the survivors to its shores...

BURN

WARREN ELLIS writer • **ROGER CRUZ & RENATO ARLEM** pencils
with help from **CHARLES MOTA & EDDIE WAGNER**
PHIL MOY, TOM WEGRZYN & HARRY CANDELARIO inks
JOE ROSAS / DIGITAL CHAMELEON colors
RICHARD STARKINGS and **COMICRAFT** letters
SUZANNE GAFFNEY editor • **BOB HARRAS** editor-in-chief

PSYCHOMETRIC CLAIRVOYANCY:

LOUDER THAN BOMBS, THAN THE NAPALM ROAR OF FLAMES EATING VERDANT PLAINS, IS THE *HISSING* OF SUPERHEATED GASES ESCAPING THE HUNDREDS OF CHARRED BODIES...

IT WAS OUR *HOME*. OUR *REFUGE*. HUMANS AND MUTANTS, LIVING TOGETHER IN *PEACE*. NO POGROMS, NO INTOLERANCE, JUST A SHARED WISH FOR FREEDOM...

...AND A SHARED FEAR OF *APOCALYPSE*...

A thousand miles away from there, southwest of the altered states –

– the submarine recently loosed from beneath GHOST DANCE, carrying a hundred refugees along the first stage of the secret route to AVALON.

A hundred refugees – and KURT DARKHOLME –

– who are wondering if they'll ever see the sun again.

THE AIR CONDITIONING UNIT'S BLOWN! NO FILTRATION OR AIR MOVEMENT!

DO SOMETHING!

WE'RE CHOKING TO **DEATH** IN OUR OWN EXHALATIONS!

WE JUST BROKE AIR! GET THOSE PEOPLE *OUT* OF THERE!

WE *CAN'T*, WALT!

WHAT?

THE CARGO BAY *DOORS* ARE CLOSED *ELECTRICALLY!* WHEN THE ELECTRICAL SYSTEMS *BLEW*, THEY *LOCKED SOLID!*

WE'RE LOOKING FOR A *CUTTING TORCH* WITH ENOUGH *GAS* IN IT, OR A *POWER-PACK* TO *KICK-START* THE DOOR MOTORS —

— BUT I THINK THEY'RE *DEAD* IN THERE! I'M *SORRY!* I'M —

SHIP AHOY!

FIRE A *FLARE*, MAN!

WHAT? YOU CAN'T *DO* THAT!

RIGHT NOW, WE *DON'T GET* CHOICES.

KOFF! KOFF!

SHIFT SOME LEAD THERE! HELP THESE PEOPLE!

DEAD MOMMY'S DEAD SHE WON'T WAKE UP

WHERE'S DARKHÖLME?

Outside.

Kurt Darkhölme is a teleporter. It nearly killed him, waiting until the sub broke water before escaping the cargo bay death trap.

He hated leaving the refugees to die in their own stench, but he hadn't the strength to 'port out even one of them.

His instinct was to save them, and the memory of their faces puts cracks in his heart.

But it had to be done. He has a greater mission, upon which more than a hundred souls depends...

And besides, back in AMERICA, he promised himself he would see his mother again before he died...

to remind himself of the days when life was easier and she would watch over him...

GOOD GRIEF.

IF *THIS* IS AN EXAMPLE OF THE REFUGEE PIPELINE'S *COMPETENCE*, I IMAGINE AVALON IS ENTIRELY *EMPTY.*

FFLLUUGH

MOONSTAR, WILL YOU FOR PITY'S SAKE *LEAVE WADE ALONE?!*

TRAILING THESE MORONS AND WAITING A *DOG'S AGE* FOR THEM TO GET *MOVING* AGAIN IS BAD *ENOUGH*—

— WITHOUT YOU ATTEMPTING TO PLAY THE *DISAPPEARING GRAFFITI* TRICK WITH RAZORS AND WADE'S *HEALING FACTOR!*

SORRY, DAMASK.

YEAH, RIGHT.

HOLD ON — A *SIGNAL* FROM THE *CITADEL* —

THIS IS *DAMASK* FOR THE *PALE RIDERS* RESPONDING ON *SECURITY PROTOCOL* —

THIS IS *APOCALYPSE*.

RESTATE YOUR *CURRENT ORDERS*, DAMASK.

FOLLOWING DATA GATHERED FROM *GHOST DANCE* BY *DANI* IN AN *UNDERCOVER* ROLE —

— WE ARE TO *TRAIL* THE FLIGHT OF THE *DISSIDENT KURT DARKHÖLME* ALONG THE *SECRET ROUTE* TO *AVALON*.

WE ARE THEN TO RETURN WITH AVALON'S *LOCATION*, HERETOFORE *UNKNOWN*, FOR YOUR PERSONAL *EDIFICATION* AND AMUSEMENT.

DARKHOLME IS *MAGNETO'S* CREATURE, AND THAT ONE IS *SCHEMING*.

THE MAN PLANS LIKE A *SPIDER*, HURLING HIS STRANDS OF INTRIGUE IN ALL DIRECTIONS.

I MUST BURN *ALL* EDGES OF HIS WEB. *THEREFORE*, YOUR ORDERS ARE *CHANGED*.

I AM PREPARING A *SECONDARY* EXPEDITION TO *FOLLOW* YOU. APPRISE ME OF YOUR LOCATION AT ALL TIMES.

YOU ARE TO FOLLOW THE DISSIDENT TO AVALON —

— AND *THEN* YOU ARE TO *KILL* AVALON.

I HAVE SPOKEN. ··SKRIKK··

QUIT SCREAMING, I HAVEN'T TOUCHED YOU.

YET.

I WAS JUST PLAYING —

DON'T BE MAD, DAMASK, PLEASE —

SHUT UP.

SHUT UP.

SHUT UP.

DANI? DANI?

WHY? WHY IS ALL THE BLOOD, DAMASK? WHY IS SHE ALL NOT MOVING?

BECAUSE I JUST KILLED HER.

AND I LOVED IT.

— MAIN THING, FRIENDS, IS AVOIDING DETECTION BY PATROLS. THESE DISUSED BALLAST TANKS ARE SCAN-SHIELDED.

YOUR VALUABLES WILL HELP OUR COVER — WE'RE SUPPOSED TO BE A SHIPWRECK RECOVERY VESSEL, AND THESE WILL BE OUR ALIBI IN THE EVENT OF BOARDING.

I KNOW IT'S COLD AND WET DOWN THERE — BUT IT COULD BE WORSE, RIGHT?

TRY AND RELAX. WE'LL SEE YOU ON THE OTHER SIDE.

OKAY, EVERYONE TOPSIDE. I WANT TO BE IN DEEPER WATER BEFORE WE DO THE DEED.

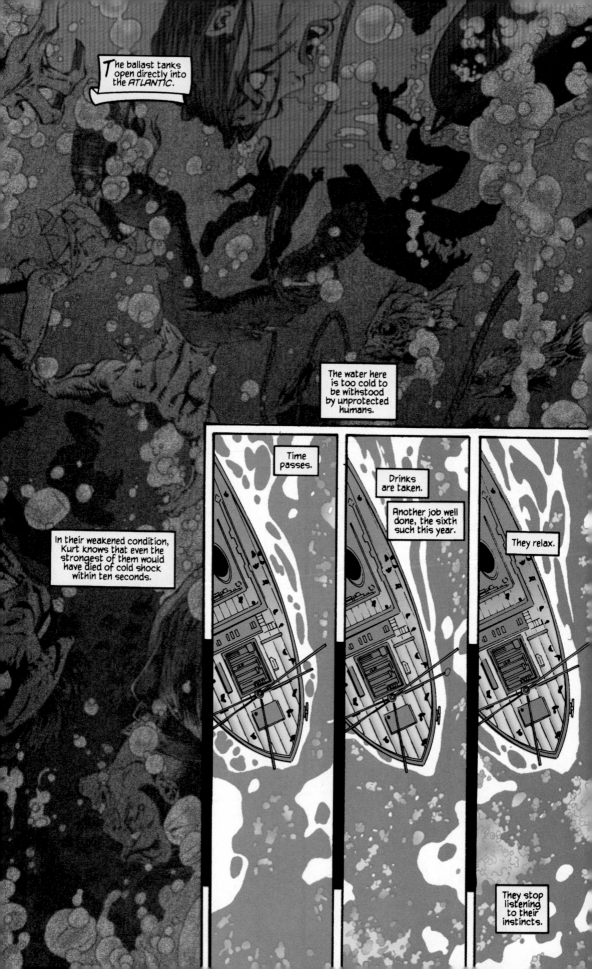

The ballast tanks open directly into the *ATLANTIC.*

The water here is too cold to be withstood by unprotected humans.

In their weakened condition, Kurt knows that even the strongest of them would have died of cold shock within ten seconds.

Time passes.

Drinks are taken.

Another job well done, the sixth such this year.

They relax.

They stop listening to their instincts.

And they don't realize what they've drifted into until it's too late.

Some time ago, APOCALYPSE came to the understanding that the American Subcontinent, large as it is, could no longer cope with the amount of corpses he was creating.

So he had the decomposing overspill located to small islands across the Atlantic.

ATROCITY ZONES.

X'd FROM SOCIETY

THE PROPS ARE CLOGGED WITH STIFFS! THE BLADES'LL SHATTER IF WE TRY AND PULL OUT OF IT — WE'RE STUCK HERE UNTIL THE TIDES CHANGE!

WHO WAS MANNING THE HELM?

ME... SORT OF...

BRAPP

TOERAG.

EINARSSON! DON'T YOU *DARE* TRY AND PUT ANY REVS ON THOSE ENGINES WITHOUT MY SAY-SO!

EINARSSON? *ANSWER* ME!

FOR WHAT YOU'VE DONE...

"...YOU'RE ALL GOING TO DIE."

BAMF

WEEKES. I THINK ONE OF THE *DUMPEES* IS STILL ON BOARD.

YOU'RE IN THE WEAPONS CACHE — BE READY FOR US TO *TOOL UP*.

WEEKES?

GYAAAH!

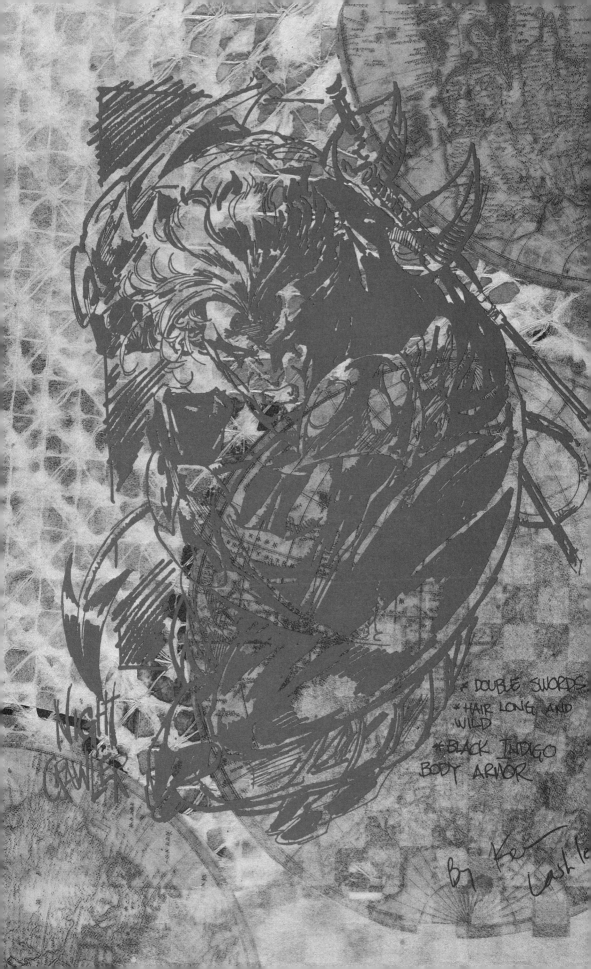

NIGHT CRAWLER

* DOUBLE SWORDS
* HAIR LONG AND WILD
* BLACK INDIGO BODY ARMOR

By Ken Lashley

AMERICA IS DEAD.

The creature APOCALYPSE stamps upon these altered states, preparing to take the world as his own. He has already won.

But still, a troubled dissident movement strives against the New World order. Once riven by failure and dispute, the revolutionary cell called X-MEN fights with new purpose. Following their discovery of a man purporting to originate from an alternate timeline, cell leader MAGNETO dispatches guerrilla fighter KURT DARKHOLME to locate the woman called DESTINY. Her mutant gene for psychometric clairvoyancy -- literally, to read the future of anyone she touches -- will validate the alternate man's claims.

To effect this, Darkholme has begun the dangerous journey along a secret refugee pipeline from America to Destiny's location, the hidden refuge of Avalon -- to the shores of which survivors are ferried by his mother, the single person outside Avalon who can know Destiny by sight -- MYSTIQUE.

His voyage has been interrupted by murderous pirates, upon a ship trapped in the reef of cadavers ringing an Atrocity Zone -- a South Atlantic island upon which are piled the overspill from Apocalypse's American genocide...

STAN LEE PRESENTS A WORLD WITHOUT XAVIER

BODY HEAT

WARREN ELLIS writer • **KEN LASHLEY** pencils • **TOM WEGRZYN** (with **PHILIP MOY**) inks
JOE ROSAS / DIGITAL CHAMELEON colors • **RICHARD STARKINGS** and **COMICRAFT** letters
SUZANNE GAFFNEY editor • **BOB HARRAS** editor-in-chief

DON'T YOU TELL *ME* WHAT TO DO, *MONK* --

KURT. *WAIT.*

I AM THE *FERRY-WOMAN* OF THE *INFERNAL GALLOP,* AND I MUST SPEAK WITH *DESTINY.* WHY ISN'T SHE HERE TO *MEET* US?

IRENE HAS GROWN *FRAIL.* WHEN THE PASSING OF YOUR BOAT TRIGGERS THE *ARRIVALS ALARMS* IN AVALON, IT IS NOW *I* WHO TRAVELS TO GREET THEM.

I AM *CAIN.*

THEN THAT MEANS *YOU* GET TO CARRY THE *CRATES.* LET'S MOVE *OUT.*

Kurt hears his mother make a small noise as her toes touch *AVALON* for the first time.

As they move off, it doesn't get much easier for her.

Destiny, with a little pained noise she might've learned from Raven, turns and walks away.

The others follow. Nowhere else to go.

Avalon Village.

THIS PLACE IS *LOVELY*, BUT IT *DOESN'T* MAKE UP FOR THE LAST HOUR'S *SILENCE*, IRENE...

COME IN AND SIT DOWN. WE NEED TO *TALK* BEFORE YOU *LEAVE*.

RAVEN, I'D LIKE TO INTRODUCE YOU TO OUR MOST *RECENT* ARRIVAL.

I DON'T *KNOW* HER *REAL* NAME, AS SHE *INSISTS* ON BEING CALLED *SWITCHBACK*.

THE DAY SHE CAME, I *READ HER FUTURE*.

WE'RE ALL GOING TO *DIE*.

SO MUCH FOR *AMATEUR PSYCHOLOGY*, SON.

JUST BE GLAD HE CROAKED *AFTER* HE CARRIED MY INSURANCE HERE.

WHAT HAPPENED?

BEST GUESS? DRIVE AN ALMOST *PSYCHOPATHIC NEED* FOR PEACE UP HARD AGAINST A DEEP-SEATED *LUST* FOR *VIOLENCE* -- HE'S HAD AN *ANEURISM.* COULDN'T STAND THE STRAIN AND A BRAIN VEIN POPPED.

LIFE *STINKS.* I'M DOING THEM ALL A *FAVOR.*

WHY AREN'T YOU USING YOUR *POWERS,* DAMASK? THEY ALL NEED TO BE KILLED, APOCALYPSE *SAYS.*

AMERICA IS DEAD.

The creature APOCALYPSE stamps upon these altered states, preparing to take the world as his own. He has already won.

But still, a troubled dissident movement strives against the New World Order. Once riven by failure and dispute, the revolutionary cell called X-MEN fights with renewed purpose. Following their discovery of a man purporting to originate from an alternate timeline, cell leader MAGNETO dispatches guerrilla fighter KURT DARKHOLME to locate the woman called DESTINY. Her mutant gene for psychometric clairvoyancy -- literally, to read the future of anyone she touches -- will validate the alternate man's claims.

To effect this, Darkholme has begun the dangerous journey along a secret refugee pipeline from America to Destiny's location, the hidden refuge of AVALON -- to the shores of which survivors are ferried by his mother, the single person outside Avalon who knows Destiny by sight -- MYSTIQUE.

They were trailed by Apocalypse's covert striketeam, THE PALE RIDERS. The leader, DAMASK, has experienced a moral earthquake upon entering Avalon, and switched sides on the point of destroying the place under Apocalypse's orders.

But worse than her are coming to make scorched earth of the refuge...

ON FIRE

WARREN ELLIS writer • **KEN LASHLEY** pencils • **TOM WEGRZYN** (with **PHILIP MOY**) inks
JOE ROSAS colors • **RICHARD STARKINGS** and **COMICRAFT** letters
DIGITAL CHAMELEON separations
SUZANNE GAFFNEY editor • **BOB HARRAS** editor-in-chief

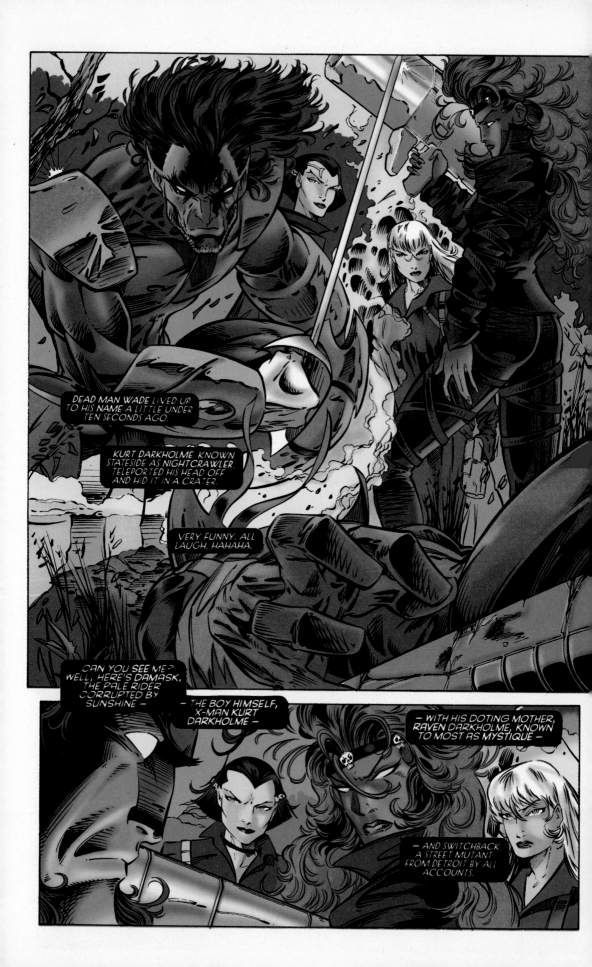

LET'S GET BACK TO THE VILLAGE, START ALL OVER AGAIN WITH DESTINY. COME ON, KURT — WE *STILL* HAVE TO *CONVINCE* HER TO *RETURN* TO *AMERICA* WITH YOU.

IN A MINUTE.

NOW — WHAT'S APOCALYPSE SENDING? SENTINELS? A TROOP OF *INFINITES?*

I DON'T *KNOW.* HONESTLY. HE NEVER *SAID.*

COME HERE.

YES. THAT'S IT.

CAN YOU SEE ME YET?

JUST AS I THOUGHT. LIKE *VELVET.*

COME ON.

POINT *TWO:* THERE'S *NO* WAY MOM'S GOING TO LEAVE AVALON ON THE SAY-SO OF A *PROBABLE PIRATE* —

— PITCHING SOME *CRAZY* STORY ABOUT *ALTERNATE WORLDS*, SO —

AND YOU HAVEN'T SEEN *WEIRDER?*

WHAT DO YOU MEAN?

OKAY. *AMERICA* IS *RULED* BY SOME *PRIMAL FORCE* FOR *DARWINISM.* THERE'S A *BAR* IN *MANHATTAN* RUN BY A GUY WITH *WINGS.*

IN THE MIDDLE OF *ANTARCTICA* THERE'S A *WARM PARADISE* WHERE MUTANTS AND HUMANS *CO-EXIST* IN *PEACE.*

AND *MAGNETO'S* GOT A GUY WHO *MIGHT* COME FROM A *DIFFERENT REALITY* WHERE APOCALYPSE NEVER CAUGHT *HOLD* OF THINGS.

YOU TELL *ME* WHICH ONE SOUNDS LIKE A CRAZY STORY, DOUG.

ALL THAT WE IN *X-CALIBRE* ARE *SAYING,* YOUNG DOUGLAS BOY, IS GIVE US A CHANCE TO *CONFIRM* SAID CRAZY STORY.

HA. X-CALIBRE?

KURT'S NAMED AFTER A *BULLET.* *REMEMBER* THAT.

And, in the midst of it all, stands *DESTINY*, she who **built** this haven of peaceful co-existence.

In the eye of the storm, watching *RAVEN'S* team try to contain it all, she is torn.

Shouldn't **she**, too, be **fighting** for her **dream**? Surely a dream is **worth** fighting for?

Why, then, does she so desperately want to **run**?

NO NO NO NO. I WANT TO HANG AROUND A WHILE. I WANT TO HAVE SOME WRONG FUN WITH YOU.

And with a shock she realizes... without ever stepping foot on the soil of *AVALON*, *APOCALYPSE* has come...

...and *DESTINY* cannot help but feel the blood on her hands.

For in this world, no promises of sanctuary can be kept.

The psionic skinning blades jab deep into the folds of the mutant's brain.

Damask **twists** them selectively, paralyzing speech centers, movement functions, chemical producers —

— rendering this host **impossible** for the *SHADOW KING* to inhabit.

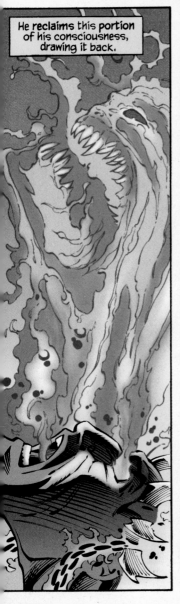

He **reclaims** this **portion** of his consciousness, drawing it back.

BLAST. I MISSED SHADOW KING AND CAUGHT THE *HOST BODY'S* MIND *INSTEAD.*

YOU **ACTUALLY** CAUGHT HIS *MIND* BETWEEN THOSE **BLADES?**

YEAH. I GUESS I GOT A LITTLE OVER-ZEALOUS. YOUR **MOTHER'S** GOING TO HAVE MY HIDE.

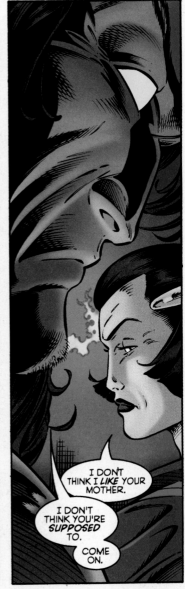

I DON'T THINK I *LIKE* YOUR MOTHER.

I DON'T THINK YOU'RE *SUPPOSED* TO.

COME ON.

HER MEMORIES SPILL OUT BETWEEN MY SHARP, SHARP FINGERS, EACH ONE IMPRINTING ON HER CLEVER FLESH.

DELICIOUS.

THE WOMAN'S A SHAPESHIFTER.

IT'S QUITE AN EXHILARATING FORM OF TORTURE.

AND THERE'S ONE MEMORY WORSE THAN ALL THE REST...

KKKK
K

KKHHUUUR

There. A video flicker. An electric sketch in the night.

A thing of pure mind, travelling in a realm of ghosts and wild physics.

Caught in the ecstasy of *MYSTIQUE'S* agony, the *SHADOW KING* notices their presence a second too late.

The partners fate dealt *KURT* move as one —

— *DAMASK* spins out the snaring **chain** of her mind, as *SWITCHBACK* forces her **timefield** to its limit —

— and together, they reduce the **filthy** intellect of the *SHADOW KING* to wet, hissing shreds.

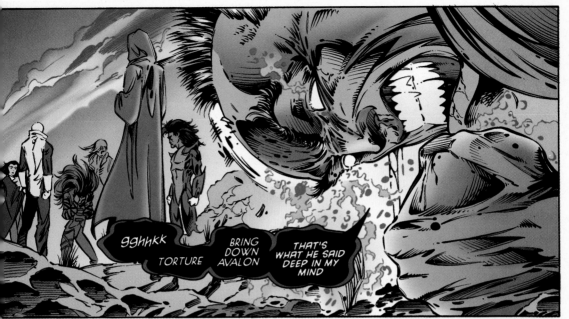

gghhkk

TORTURE

BRING
DOWN
AVALON

THAT'S
WHAT HE SAID
DEEP IN MY
MIND

BRING
DOWN
AVALON

DOUG RAMSEY moves
on instinct. His head
still full of KURT
DARKHOLME'S words.

He takes his head
out of the sand.

He faces the real
world head on.

Life out
of death.

And he sees what
the dream can
achieve.

I...
...I THOUGHT THIS WAS THE ONLY PLACE WHERE MY DREAM COULD SURVIVE, RAVEN.

PERHAPS, IF I HAD PLANTED MY HOPES IN DIFFERENT FIELDS...

...PERHAPS, PERHAPS AND MAYBES, GAMES WE PLAY WITH OURSELVES...

...PERHAPS APOCALYPSE CAN BE PREVENTED FROM BURNING MORE DREAMS.

ALL RIGHT, NIGHTCRAWLER. I'M COMING WITH YOU.

TAKE ME BACK TO MAGNETO AND THE X-MEN.

AND I SWEAR BY ALL I HOLD HOLY... WE WILL BRING DOWN THE HIGH LORD APOCALYPSE.

TO BE CONCLUDED IN X-MEN OMEGA